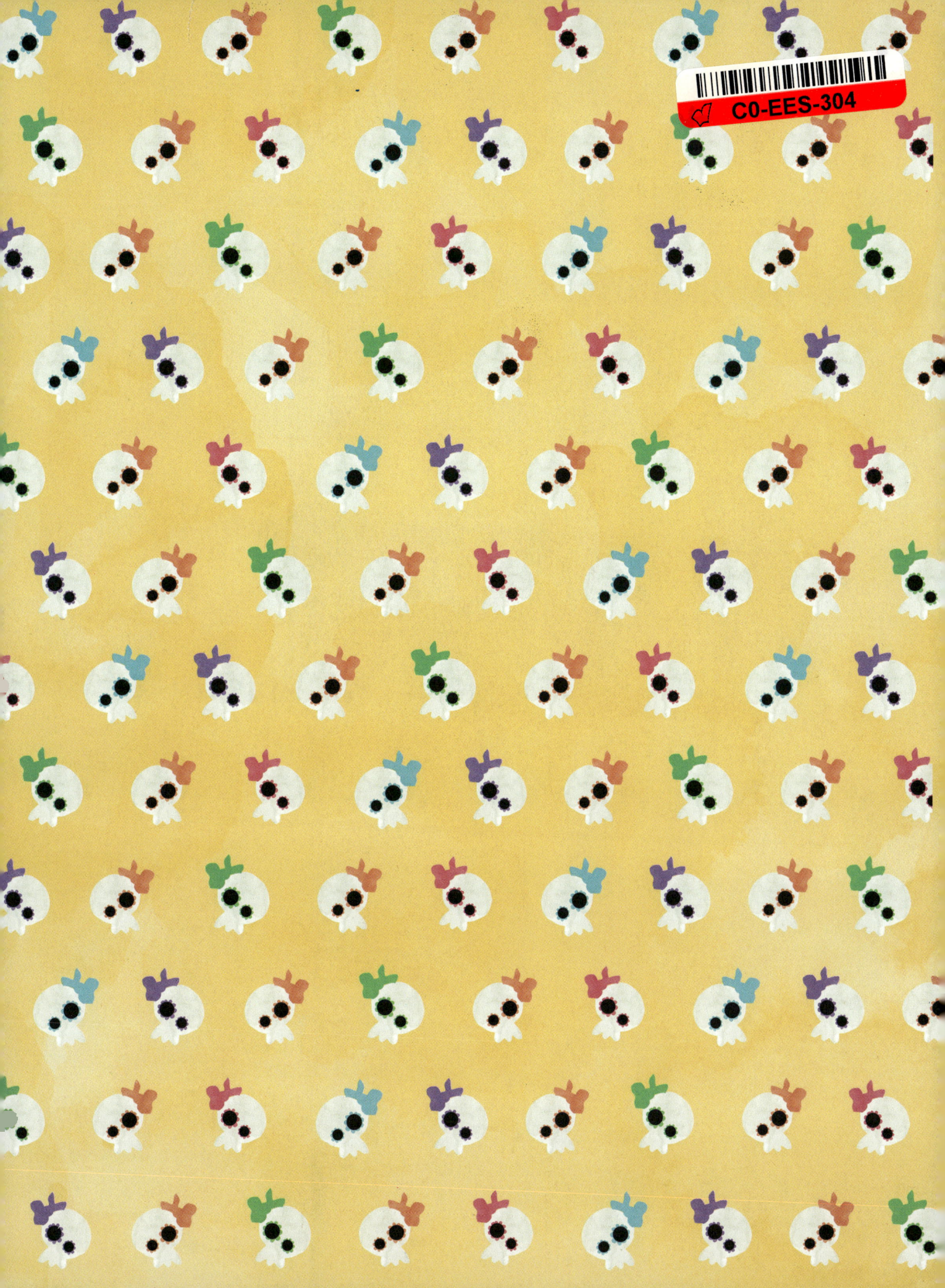

THIS BOOK BELONGS TO
_____

To my Dad, who made sure that all my life was full of marvelous roller coaster rides,

to Adriana, who believed that all this made sense,

to Mando, who had the best idea yet!

No part of this publication may be reproduced, stored in a retrieval system, or transmitted in any form or by any means, electronic, mechanical, photocopying, recording, or otherwise, without written permission of the publisher. For information regarding permission, write to Worldwide Buddies Corp., 275 Madison Avenue, Suite 801, New York, NY 10016.

ISBN 978-1-338-60244-9

Text and illustrations copyright © 2018 by Worldwide Buddies Ltd. All rights reserved. Published by Scholastic Inc., 557 Broadway, New York, NY 10012, by arrangement with Worldwide Buddies. SCHOLASTIC and associated logos are trademarks and/or registered trademarks of Scholastic Inc.

The publisher does not have any control over and does not assume any responsibility for author or third-party websites or their content.

12 11 10 9 8 7   23 24

Printed in the U.S.A.   40

First Scholastic printing, September 2019

A Marvelous Mexican Misunderstanding

evi triantafyllides

illustrated by nefeli malekou

SCHOLASTIC INC.

ADRI WAS HORRIFIED.

He had been dreading this day for the past few months, ever since they moved back to Mexico.

And now, day by day, it was getting closer and closer at an alarming rate.

He could see it in people's eyes...

He could sense it in the atmosphere on the streets...

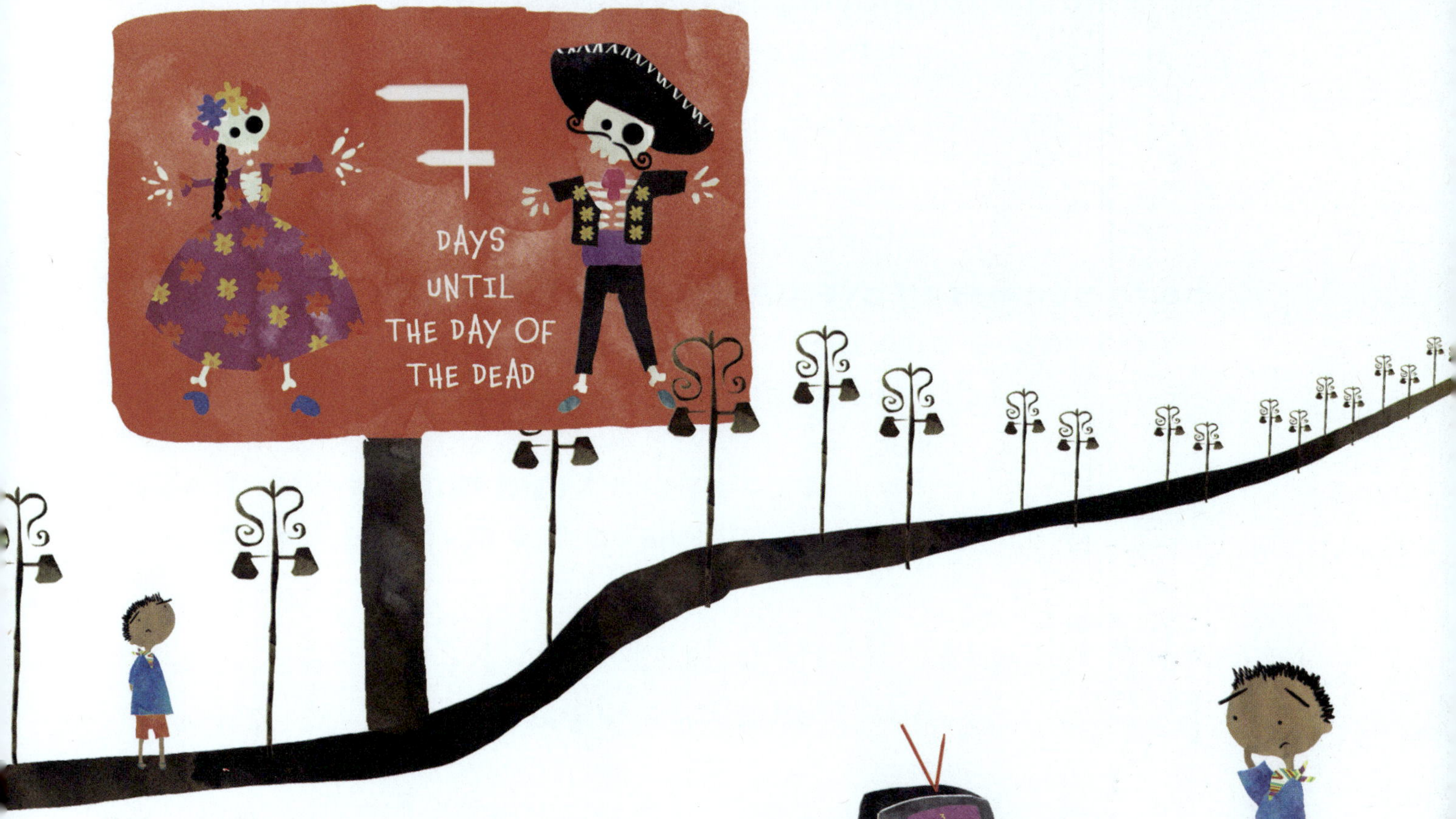
7
DAYS
UNTIL
THE DAY OF
THE DEAD

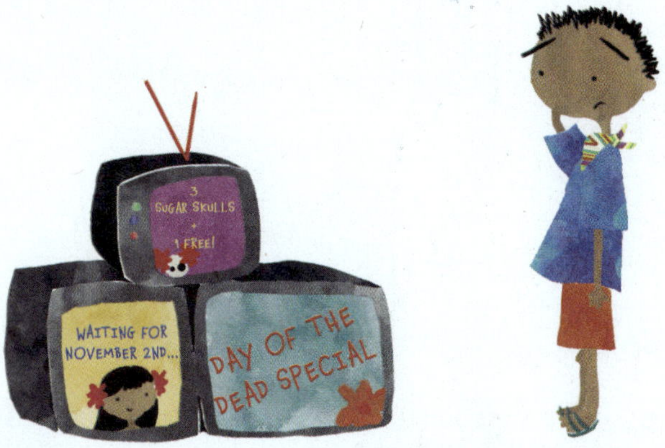
3
SUGAR SKULLS
+
1 FREE!
WAITING FOR
NOVEMBER 2ND...
DAY OF THE
DEAD SPECIAL

He could read it on every billboard
and every screen he turned to.

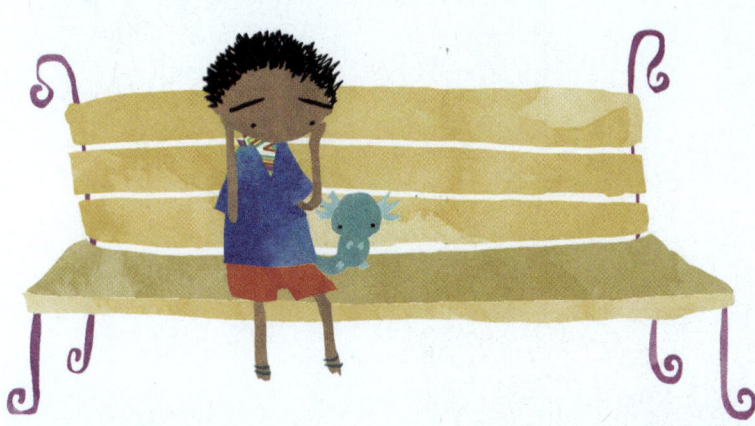

It was just impossible to escape from!

The memory kept playing in his head, over and over...
and over again.

"Oh I'm so glad you're back,"
he remembered overhearing Aunt Chiquita say to Mom.
"And you're also back in time for the Day of the Dead.
Adri will finally get to be part of it!"

"Yes, I haven't told him any details yet.
I want to keep it a surprise," Mom said.

WHAT! WHAT DEAD? WHAT SURPRISE?
Adri thought to himself.

"I got him a book on the Aztecs.
This will explain everything.
I will give it to him when the time is right,"
Mom continued.

"Hey, hey, hey, why are you hiding?"
his sister, Tani, ran up to him.

"Who are the Aztecs?
What's the Day of the Dead? How will I be part of it?
Does that mean that I am... going to... die?!"
he asked anxiously.

"Oh!! Well..." she thought for a second.
Yes. YES! OF COURSE YOU ARE GOING TO DIE!
Tani responded with excitement,
as she jumped at the opportunity to tease him.

I'M TOO YOUNG TO DIE!

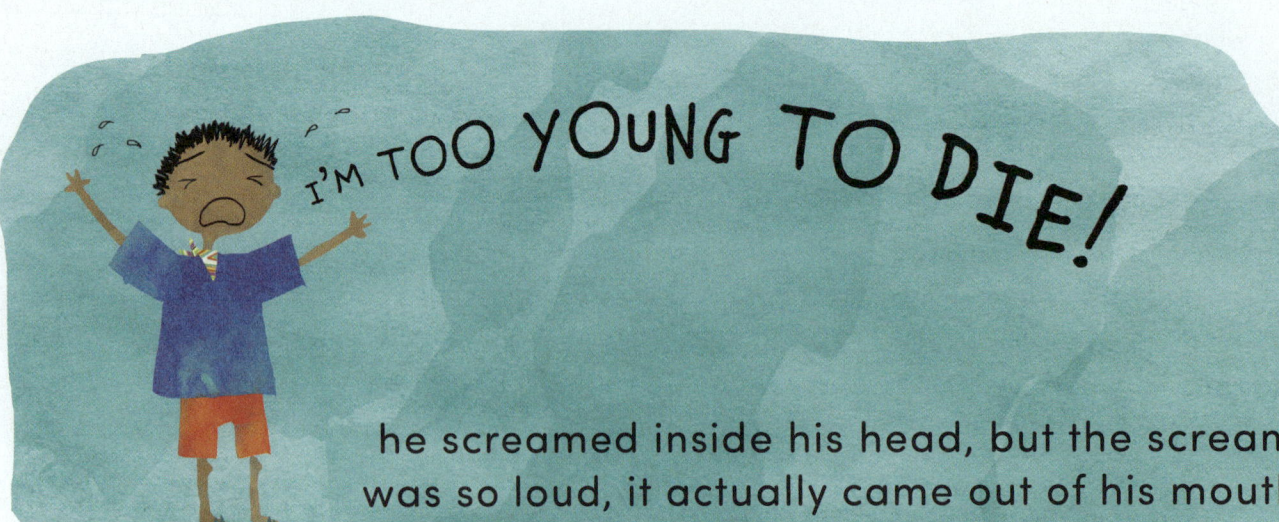

he screamed inside his head, but the scream was so loud, it actually came out of his mouth.

"But you are going to. And there's nothing you can do about it!"

"Tani. Stop teasing your brother. And Adri, enough of this. Go clean your room or you won't be able to join the celebrations this weekend."

"In that case, I'm never cleaning my room. I will open the cupboards and throw everything on the floor."

YOU'RE GOING TO DIE, YOU'RE GOING TO DIE!

"How do I know that you're not lying? You say Hermelindo doesn't love me, but toys can't speak. You say you have special witch powers, but you don't."

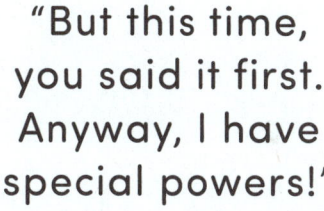

"But this time, you said it first. Anyway, I have special powers!"

"Why does Mom say that you're teasing, then?"

"She's Mom, DUH. She wouldn't want you to be sad on your last days on earth."

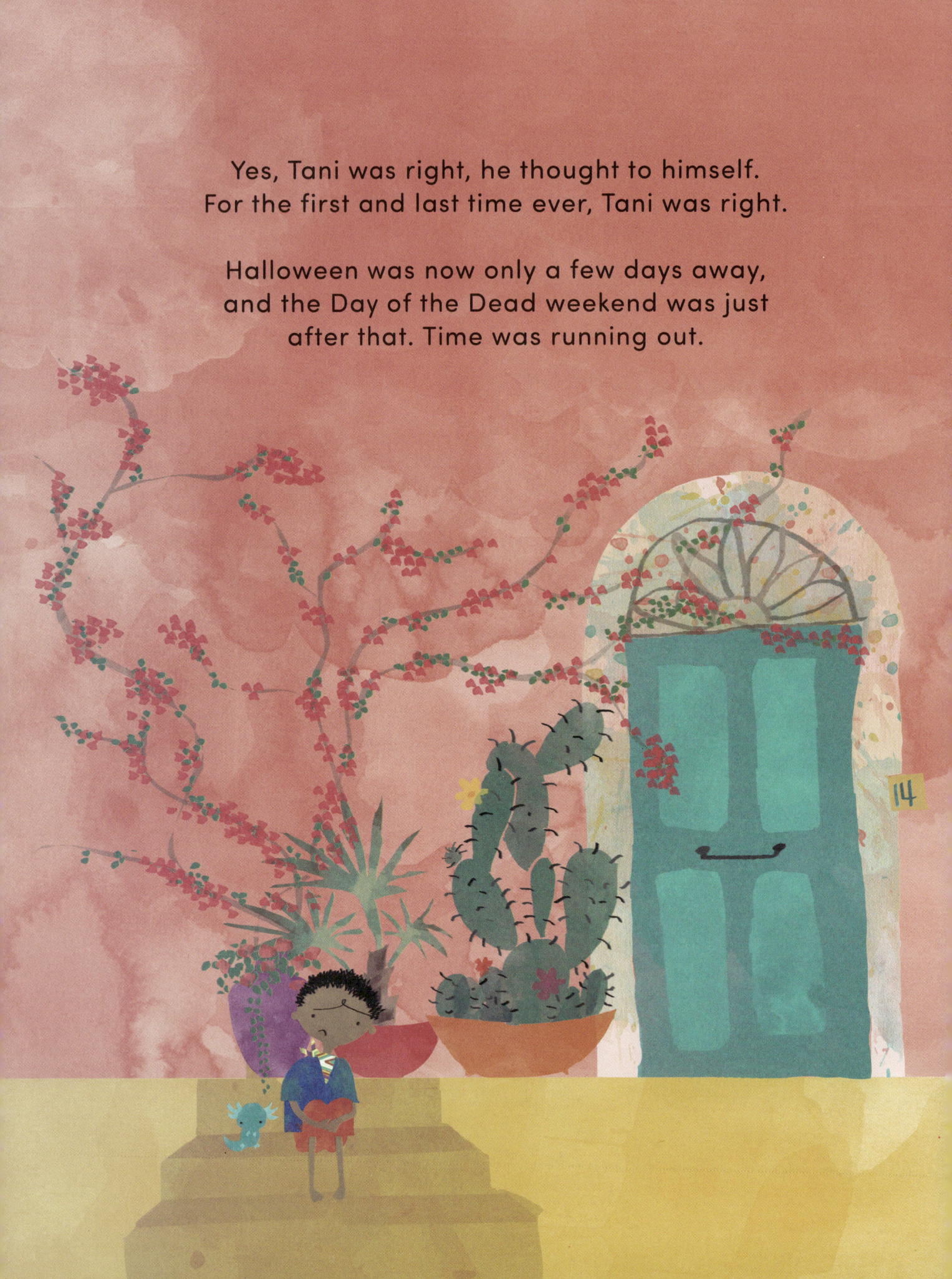

Yes, Tani was right, he thought to himself.
For the first and last time ever, Tani was right.

Halloween was now only a few days away, and the Day of the Dead weekend was just after that. Time was running out.

And every day,
the reminders kept getting worse...

"I brought Pan de Muerto –
Day of the Dead bread," the neighbor
said two days before Halloween.
"You were on my mind when I bought it.
I think you'll like it."

EVEN THE NEIGHBORS KNOW?

"Adri! Tani! I brought your Halloween outfits. Tani, this one's for you. I know that you've always wanted to be a magician," Dad surprised them the day before Halloween.

"Yay! Thanks Dad, you're the best. I'm never taking it off," Tani kissed him on the cheek.

"Adri, you never told me what outfit you'd like, so I decided a skeleton is the most appropriate."

GULP. He froze. Ok, he got it, he was going to die. He didn't need constant reminders.

"I'm making Calabaza en Tacha – your favorite,"
Mom said proudly on Halloween.
"I know how much you love it, and it couldn't be more suitable for the occasion."

"See? What did I tell you?" Tani whispered in his ear.
"She is trying to keep you happy."

"Always keep your favorite for the end,"
Mom's advice echoed in Adri's head.
"That way, the memory will last."

That's what she was doing now!
The Day of the Dead was starting tomorrow.
She was preparing his last dish.

THINGS WERE STARTING TO GET REAL.

That night, his mind couldn't stop racing.

Why was everyone being insensitive?
How could they not be sad?
Why were they so festive?!

They'd see though.
They would all miss him terribly!

I MISS YOU
GREATEST BROTHER
OF ALL TIMES!

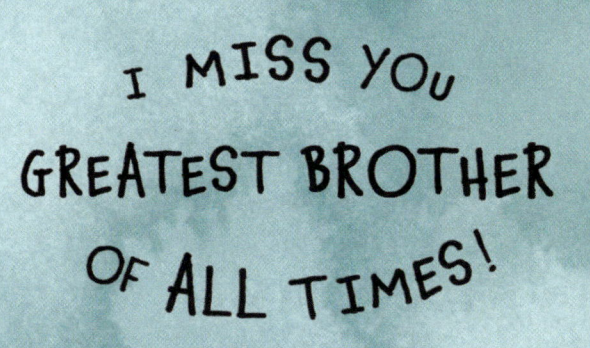

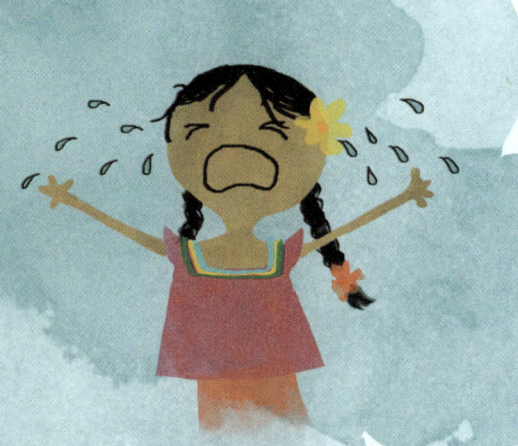

But it wasn't just his family.

The next morning, the big day arrived
and yet another surprise was waiting for him.

Everyone was out in the streets,
with faces painted like skulls.
They were talking, laughing, cheering!

"Look at all these people celebrating," Mom pointed out as they squeezed their way through the crowds.

12...54...100.. POSSIBLY 1000 PEOPLE AND EVEN MORE. THE ENTIRE CITY WAS MAKING FUN OF HIM!

"Adri, what's wrong? Why are you so upset? You know how much we love you, don't you? I know that moving was difficult, but we really do want the best for you."

He couldn't understand how this was best for him, but hearing his mom say that she loved him was all he needed at that point. And just like that, he gave her the biggest hug he'd ever given.

"I'm sure you'll have a wonderful time tonight. The entire family is taking the boat to the island of Janitzio, one of the loveliest places in the world! Just make sure you finish your homework first," Mom continued, as they walked home.

NO MORE TIME FOR CRYING.

The Day of the Dead celebrations only lasted for two days so he had to act fast. It was time to face his fate and make the final arrangements.

He opened his extremely precious diary, the one his grandmother had given him before she passed away, carefully took out two pieces of paper and started writing. His grandmother had instructed not to use it except in the most extraordinary of cases, but this was a very extraordinary case, indeed.

On the first piece of paper, he wrote:

MY GOODBYE LETTER

I CANNOT UNDERSTAND WHY YOU WANT ME TO DIE! I'M SUCH A GOOD BOY.

I ALWAYS TIDY UP MY ROOM. WELL... MAYBE SOMETIMES, IF IT'S TOO UNTIDY, I HIDE A COUPLE OF THINGS UNDER THE BED, BUT STILL, IT LOOKS TIDY, AND IF YOU THINK ABOUT IT, THAT'S WHAT YOU ASK FOR.

AND MY HOMEWORK IS ALWAYS DONE ON TIME. WELL... I GUESS IT'S TIME TO CONFESS THAT YESTERDAY I COPIED MY HOMEWORK FROM PABLO, BUT I STILL WROTE IT IN MY OWN HANDWRITING AND PUT MY NAME ON IT.

HMMM... MAYBE I'M MORE DIFFICULT THAN I THOUGHT, AND THAT'S WHY YOU DON'T CARE IF I DIE. BUT I WANT YOU TO KNOW THAT I FORGIVE YOU, AND I LOVE YOU, AND I WILL MISS YOU. EVEN YOU TANI! :-(

ADRI

And then, he had to take care of business.
On the second piece of paper, he wrote:

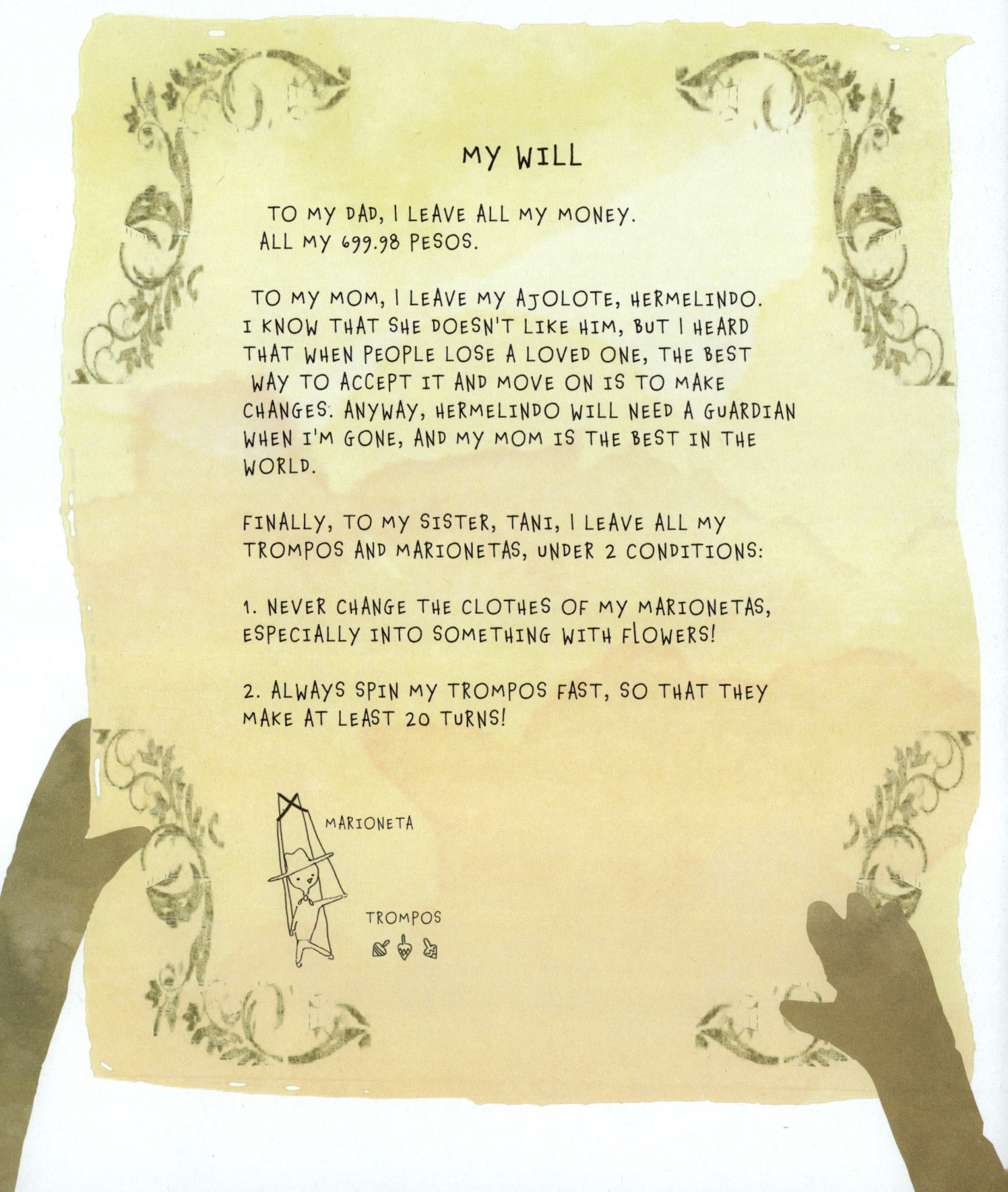

MY WILL

TO MY DAD, I LEAVE ALL MY MONEY. ALL MY 699.98 PESOS.

TO MY MOM, I LEAVE MY AJOLOTE, HERMELINDO. I KNOW THAT SHE DOESN'T LIKE HIM, BUT I HEARD THAT WHEN PEOPLE LOSE A LOVED ONE, THE BEST WAY TO ACCEPT IT AND MOVE ON IS TO MAKE CHANGES. ANYWAY, HERMELINDO WILL NEED A GUARDIAN WHEN I'M GONE, AND MY MOM IS THE BEST IN THE WORLD.

FINALLY, TO MY SISTER, TANI, I LEAVE ALL MY TROMPOS AND MARIONETAS, UNDER 2 CONDITIONS:

1. NEVER CHANGE THE CLOTHES OF MY MARIONETAS, ESPECIALLY INTO SOMETHING WITH FLOWERS!

2. ALWAYS SPIN MY TROMPOS FAST, SO THAT THEY MAKE AT LEAST 20 TURNS!

He made a complex looking signature to match the seriousness of the letters,

then folded the papers, put them in two envelopes and wrote on each one:

The ride to the island of Janitzio was the most stunning ride he had ever taken. It felt like a fairytale.
The boats were filled with people carrying flowers and offerings, and fishermen dressed in traditional outfits.

Everything was lit up by candles and there was something that made the entire setting... well, magical.

When they arrived at the island,
they walked to a graveyard.
Was it time to face his fate?

YIKES. FEAR WAS BACK.

"Isn't this wonderful?
And tomorrow you'll get to visit
Grandma," Mom whispered.

Did Mom talk to her?
How did she know he
would see Grandma?
He did miss her dearly,
but still wasn't ready to
leave his family...

Where would he
find her, anyway?
How would they talk?

Perhaps he would have to learn
the language of the Aztecs,
who had started the whole thing
in the first place!

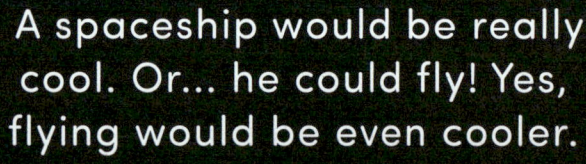

And how would he die?
Would the Aztecs pick him up?
In a canoe? An airplane?
Or maybe... a spaceship?

A spaceship would be really
cool. Or... he could fly! Yes,
flying would be even cooler.

But then again, he didn't know
how to fly. What if he fell?

"Adri! Stay close," his mom cried
as Adri moved away, lost in his thoughts.
"Take my hand. I don't want to lose you!
This is it."

OH NO! THIS WAS IT!

The crowd was standing still, looking at the sky,
as if everyone was waiting for something.
Was the Aztec spaceship coming?

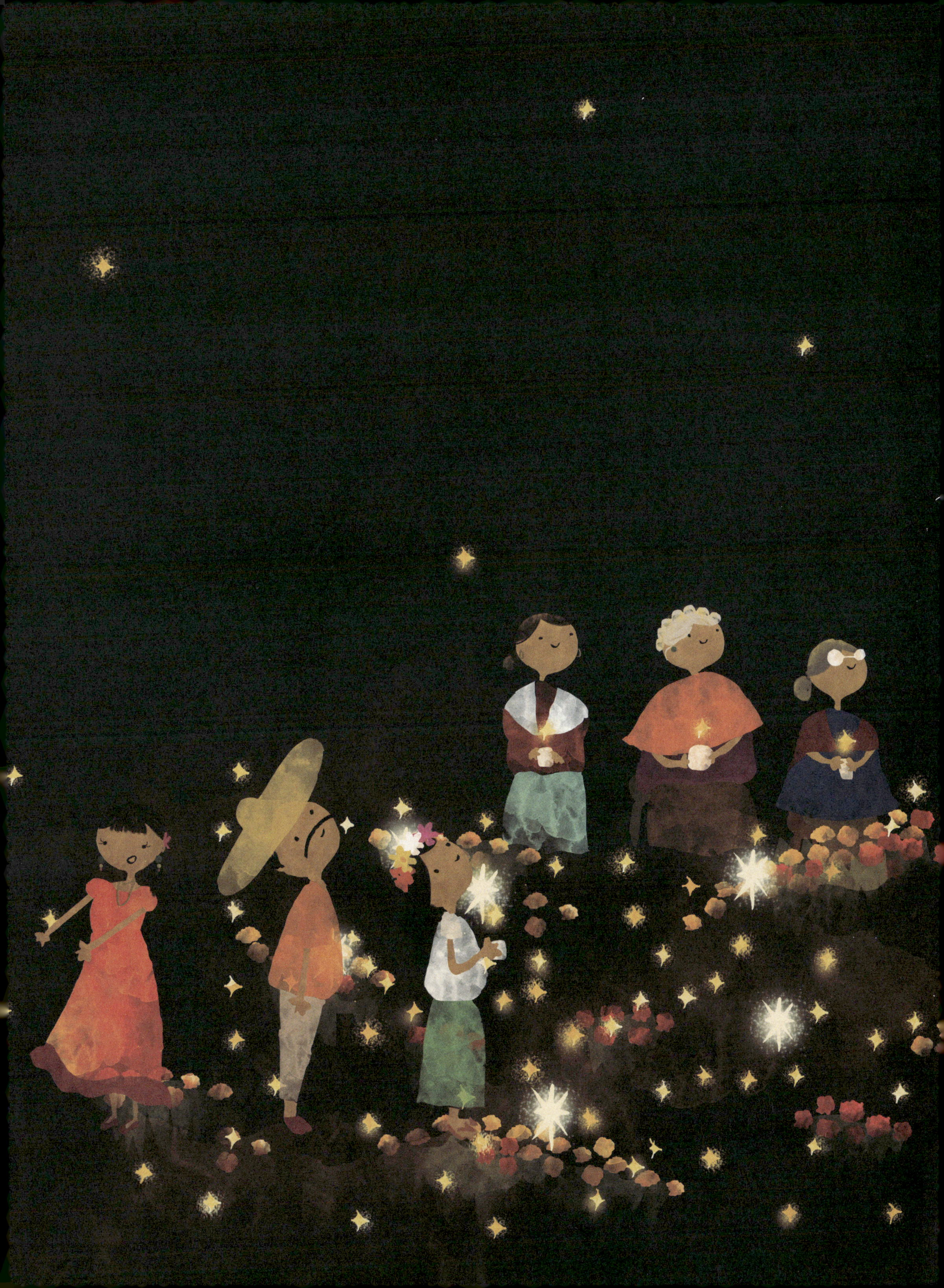

He swallowed.

His heart started beating fast. And then faster.

And faster.   It was going to explode!

NOOOooooo

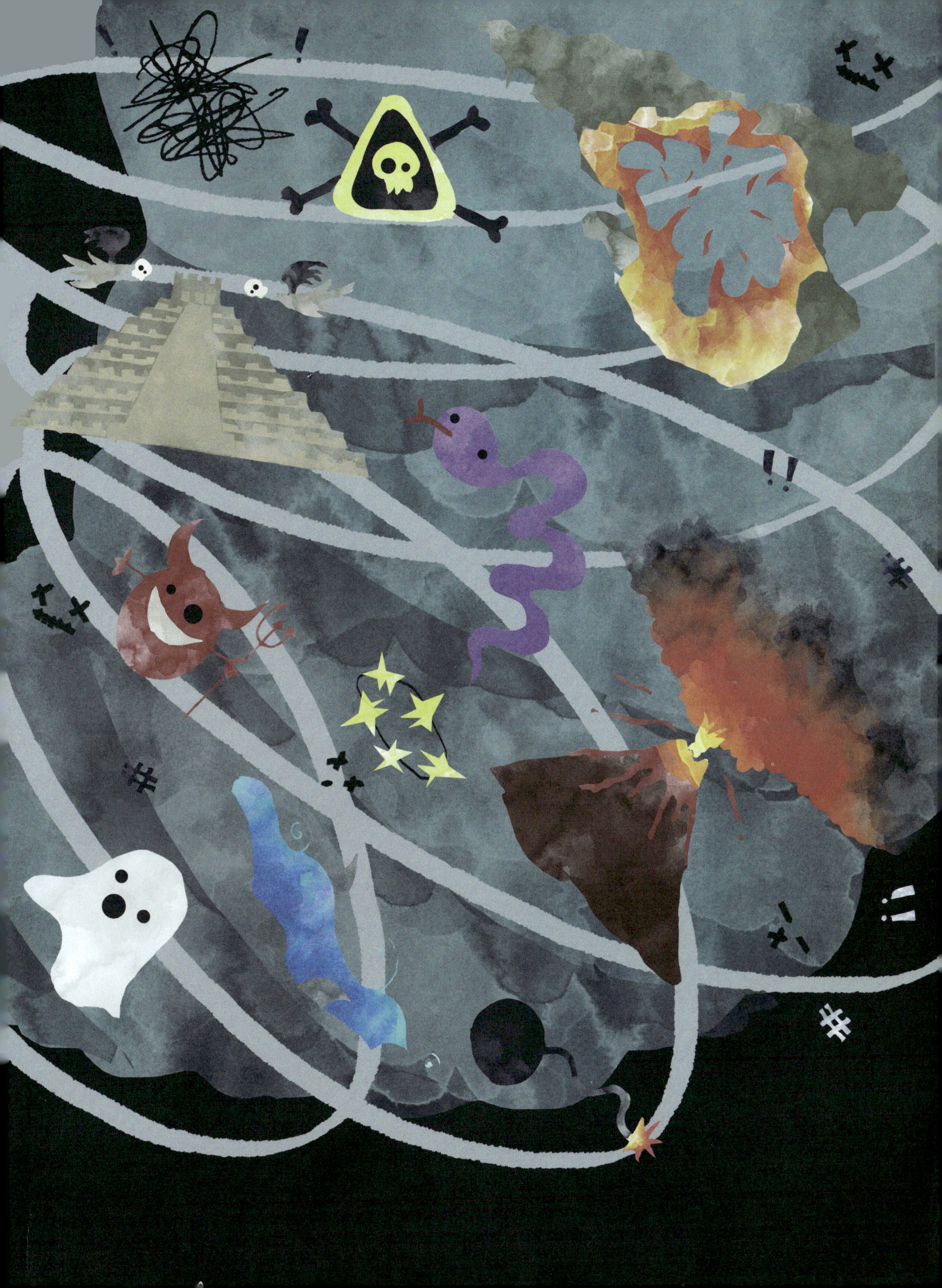

POP! CRACKLE!

SWISHHHHHH

WHAT WAS HAPPENING?

He slowly opened one eye.

He could still see Tani's braids but there was a different light to them. Then, he turned towards his Mom.

POP!

SWISHHHHHHH

POP!

She was still there.

DID HE SURVIVE?

He opened both eyes
and looked around. Hmm.
Everything seemed the same...

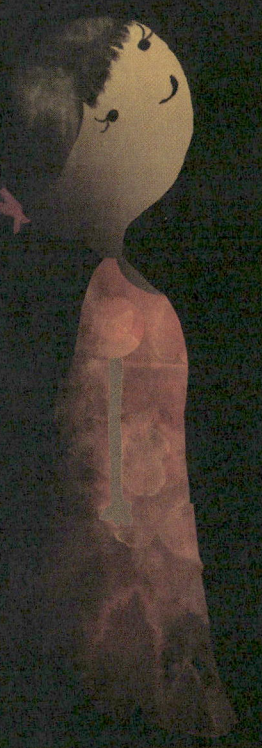

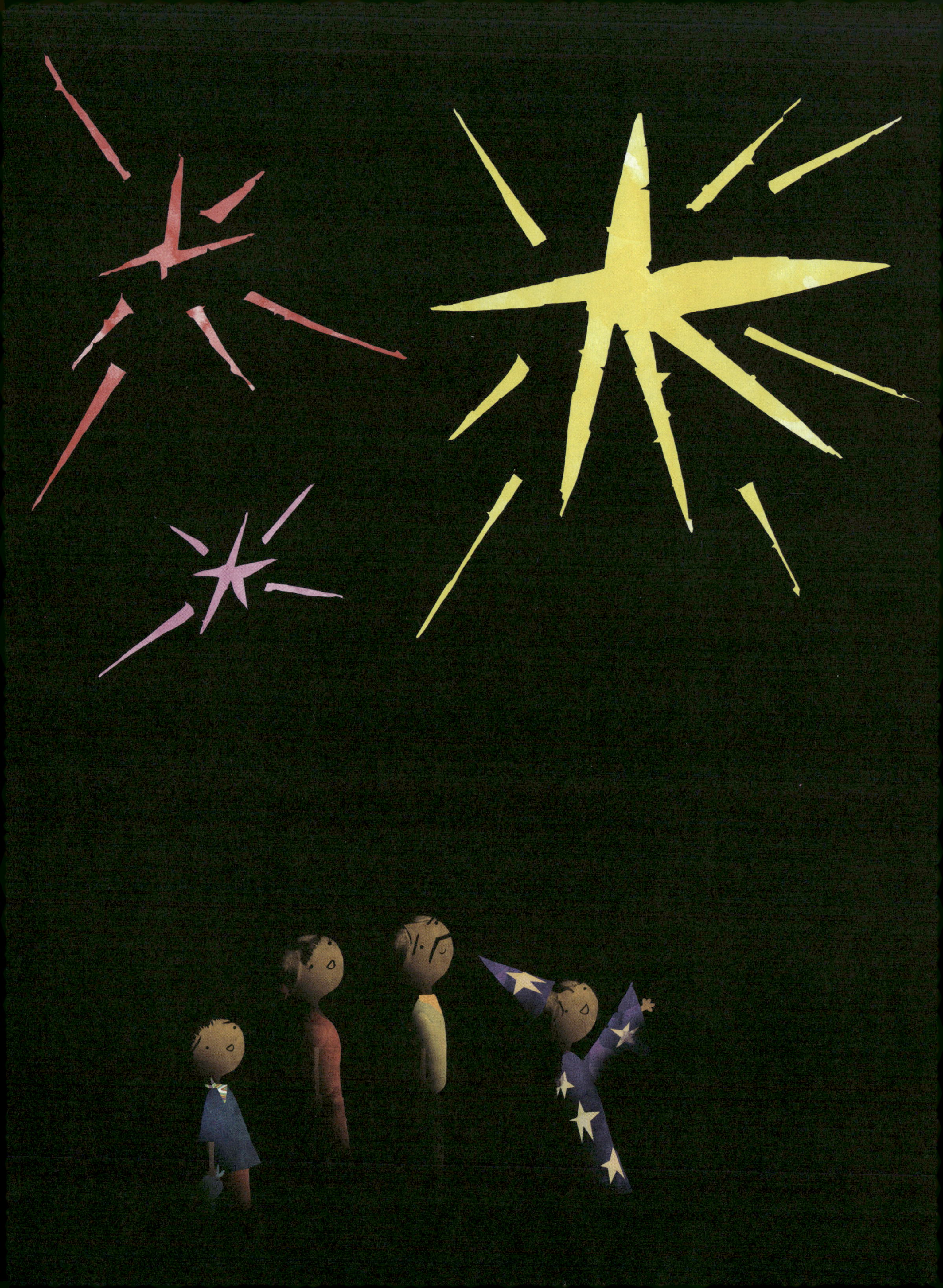

Then, looking up, he saw that the sky was filled with fireworks.
Fireworks POPPING, CRACKLING, SWISHING.

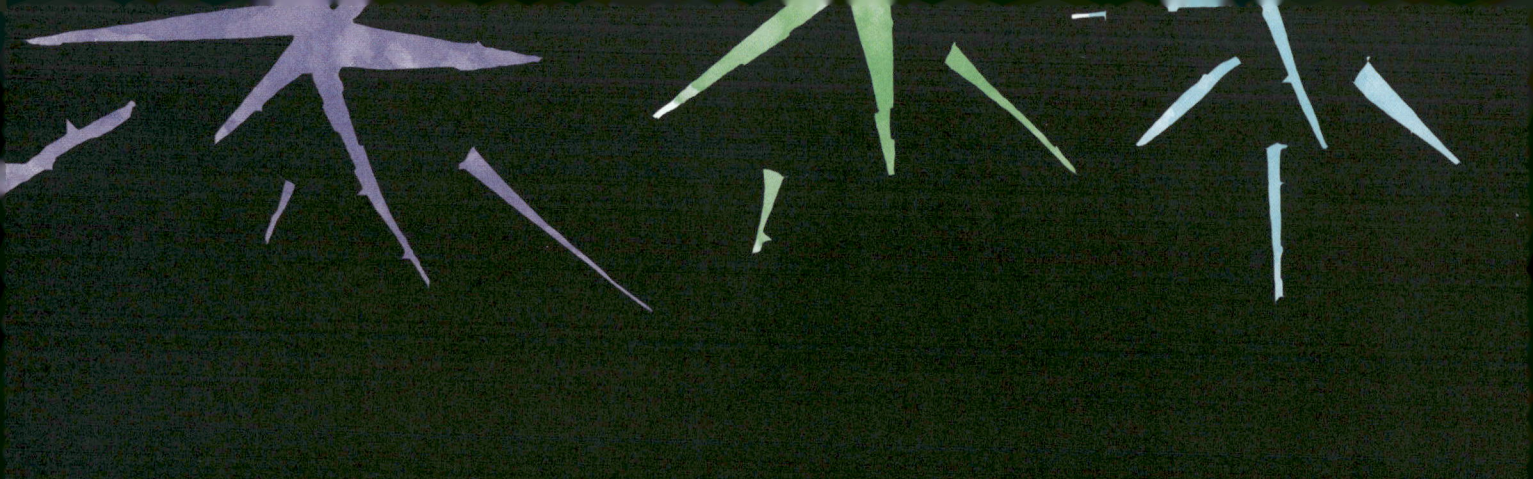

"Hey, are you still alive?"
Tani turned towards him.

"Um.." He pulled his mother's skirt.
"Mom, when am I going to die?"
he whispered, so that Tani couldn't hear him.

"Adri! You're not going to die!
What do you mean?"

"So, who's going to die?"

"No one is going to die, silly. Please stop worrying. The Day of the Dead helps us remember all those who have passed away. It's one of the happiest celebrations of the year, a time when everyone comes together to honor what we love and what we miss.

It's a reminder of what's special and important. The best way to remember all the people we've lost and cherish our precious memories with them. To remember and warm our hearts with kindness, joy and love!"

WELL, WHY DIDN'T

THEY SAY SO?!

The next day was one of the best days of his life.

In the morning, they went to church and then visited his grandmother's gravestone. Whenever they visited Abuela in the past, everyone was sad. But not that day. That day, the whole family was happy.

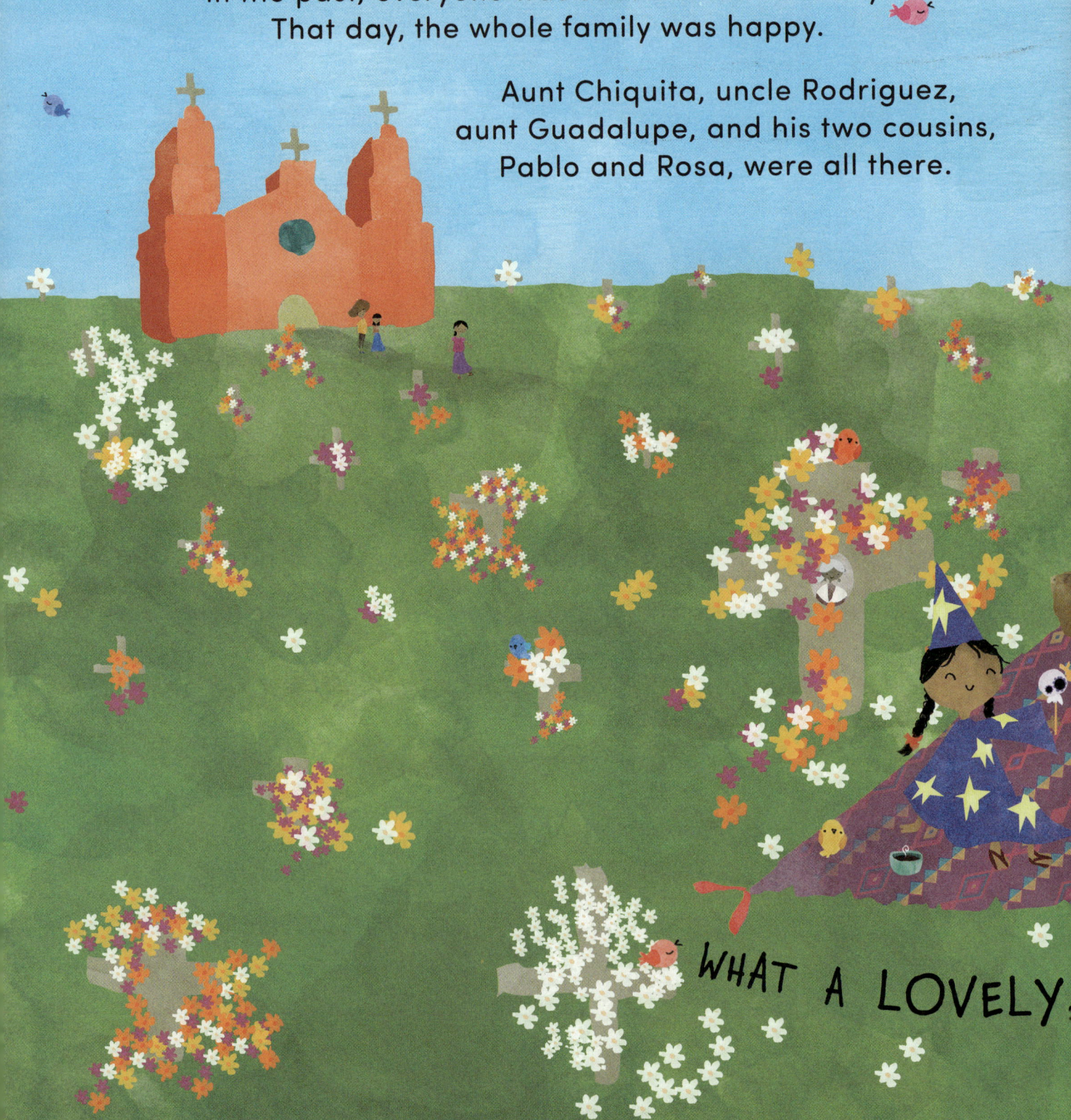

Aunt Chiquita, uncle Rodriguez, aunt Guadalupe, and his two cousins, Pablo and Rosa, were all there.

WHAT A LOVELY.

They had a marvelous picnic, ate delicious sweet sugar skulls and remembered funny stories of Grandma.

Later, at home, they all played games and laughed for hours. And while usually his mom made him go to bed early, this time, she let him stay up until midnight!

LOVELY DAY THE DAY OF THE DEAD WAS!

At night, going to his room to sleep,
he found Tani sitting on his bed.

She was holding...

HIS GOODBYE LETTER AND HIS WILL!

"Ohhh you love
me and you will
miss me!"

"Hey, give
me that!"

"Mom! Adri didn't do his homework this weekend! He copied it from Pablo!"

OH, GREAT.

SOME MARVELOUS MEXICAN MYSTERIES

1. Do you know the name of the capital city of Mexico? The name has two words, one of which is Mexico, and the other is city...

    _ _ _ _ _   _ _ _ _

2. Mexico is the 14th largest country in the world. It's so big that it falls under several time zones. Do you know how many time zones Mexico has? To find the answer, spot the page with the clocks on the wall. How many do you see?

3. The Mexican flag is green, white and red, representing independence, religion and unity. Who in the story wears clothes with the colors of the Mexican flag?

4. The Mexican currency is called peso. Do you remember how many pesos Adri had?

5. Adri's stuffed animal, Hermelindo, is an ajolote (axolotl) – the cutest water lizard that lives in Mexico and is in danger of extinction. If you had one, what would you name it? Try giving it an extra special, Mexican name!

6. Mexico introduced chocolate, corn and chillies to the world. Yum, yum and yum! On which page can you find them in the story?

CAN YOU SOLVE THEM?

7. Mexico is surrounded by the "Ring of Fire" and that's why it has lots of volcanoes and earthquakes. One of Mexico's most famous volcanoes is called Popocatepetl. Did the sound make you giggle? It definitely made us giggle! Can you try saying it without giggling?!

8. The Chihuahua is the world's smallest dog and is named after a Mexican state. Who has a Chihuahua in the book?

9. A sombrero is a typical Mexican hat that is large and round. How many can you find in the story?

10. Mexico has the largest number of pyramids in the world. The most famous one is the Chichen Itza Pyramid, which has been declared as one of the New Seven Wonders of the World. On which page can you spot it in the story?

11. The Aztecs were a civilization that lived from the 14th to the 16th century. They were famous for their agriculture, for building pyramids and temples, for creating islands on lakes, and for designing a complex calendar system. They lived on an island in Lake Texcoco. Now, that lake is none other than the capital city of Mexico, which is called...
    (you already know this!)

MY SPANISH DICTIONARY

YUMMY FOODS

Calabaza en tacha: Candied pumpkin
Calavera de azúcar: Sugar skull
Chocolate caliente: Hot chocolate
Elote: Corn cob
Empanada: Stuffed pastry
Enchilada: Stuffed tortilla roll topped with chilli
Pan de muerto: Day of the Dead bread
Tamal: Steamed food wrapped in corn husk or plantain leaves

FAMILY

Yo: Me
Madre: Mother
Padre: Father
Hermano: Brother
Hermana: Sister
Abuela: Grandmother
Abuelo: Grandfather
Tía: Aunt
Tío: Uncle

WORDS TO KNOW

Hola: Hello
Buenos días: Good morning
Buenas noches: Good night
Por favor: Please
Gracias: Thank you
De nada: You are welcome
Lo siento: I'm sorry
Adiós: Goodbye
Día de los Inocentes: Day of the Innocents
Día de los Muertos: Day of the Dead
Ofrenda: Gifts offered to the dead on the Day of the Dead

WOODEN MEXICAN TOYS

Balero: Cup-and-ball toy (ball needs to be caught by the cup)
Marioneta: Puppet that can be handled using strings
Matraca: Noise maker
Piñata: Decorated container filled with small toys
Pirinola: Hexagon with numbers for players to spin
Trompo: Spinning toy

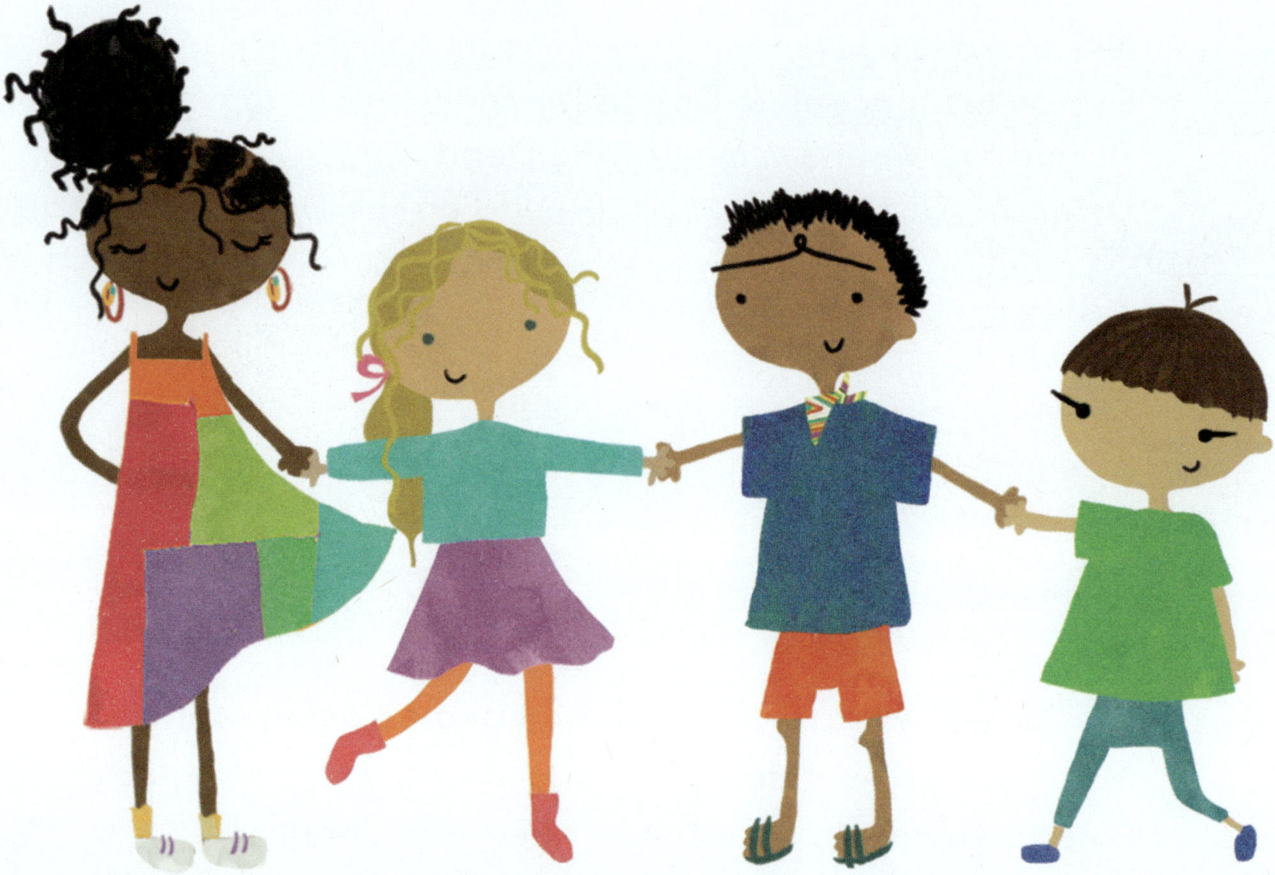

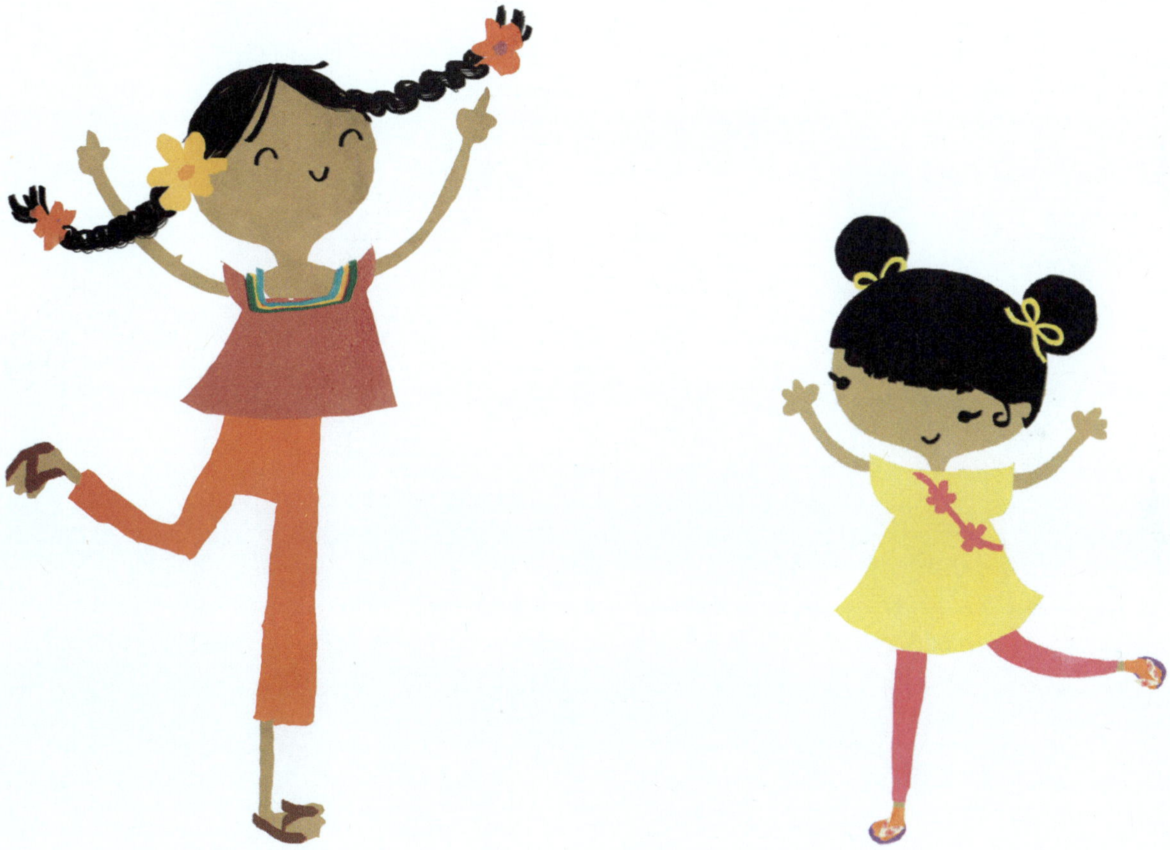